CYCLE OF THE WEREWOLF

CYCLE OF THE WEREWOLF

BY

STEPHEN KING

ILLUSTRATIONS BY
BERNI WRIGHTSON

A SIGNET BOOK

SIGNET
Published by the Penguin Group
Penguin Books USA Inc., 375 Hudson Street,
New York, New York 10014, U.S.A.
Penguin Books Ltd, 27 Wrights Lane,
London W8 5TZ, England
Penguin Books Australia Ltd, Ringwood,
Victoria, Australia
Penguin Books Canada Ltd, 10 Alcorn Avenue,
Toronto, Ontario, Canada M4V 3B2
Penguin Books (N.Z.) Ltd, 182–190 Wairau Road,
Auckland 10, New Zealand

Penguin Books Ltd, Registered Offices:
Harmondsworth, Middlesex, England

Published by Signet, an imprint of Dutton Signet,
a division of Penguin Books USA Inc.

First Signet Printing, April, 1985
13   12   11   10   9   8

Published by arrangement with The Land of Enchantment
and Stephen King

Cycle of the Werewolf was published previously in a
limited hardcover edition.

 REGISTERED TRADEMARK—MARCA REGISTRADA

Printed in the United States of America

PUBLISHER'S NOTE
This is a work of fiction. Names, characters, places, and incidents
either are the product of the author's imagination or are used
fictitiously, and any resemblance to actual persons, living or dead,
events, or locales is entirely coincidental.

In memory of Davis Grubb,
and all the voices
of Glory.

In the stinking darkness under the barn, he raised his shaggy head. His yellow, stupid eyes gleamed. *"I hunger,"* he whispered.

Henry Ellender
The Wolf

"Thirty days hath September
 April, June, and November,
 all the rest but the Second have thirty-one,
 Rain and snow and jolly sun,
 and the moon grows fat in every one."

Child's rime

JANUARY
FEBRUARY
MARCH
APRIL
MAY
JUNE
JULY
AUGUST
SEPTEMBER
OCTOBER
NOVEMBER
DECEMBER

Somewhere, high above, the moon shines down, fat and full—but here, in Tarker's Mills, a January blizzard has choked the sky with snow. The wind rams full force down a deserted Center Avenue; the orange town plows have given up long since.

Arnie Westrum, flagman on the GS&WM Railroad, has been caught in the small tool-and-signal shack nine miles out of town; with his small, gasoline-powered rail-rider blocked by drifts, he is waiting out the storm there, playing Last Man Out solitaire with a pack of greasy Bicycle cards. Outside the wind rises to a shrill scream. Westrum raises his head uneasily, and then looks back down at his game again. It is only the wind, after all . . .

But the wind doesn't scratch at doors . . . and whine to be let in.

He gets up, a tall, lanky man in a wool jacket and railroad coveralls, a Camel cigarette jutting from one corner of his mouth, his seamed New England face lit in soft orange tones by the kerosene lantern which hangs on the wall.

The scratching comes again. Someone's dog, he thinks, lost and wanting to be let in. That's all it is . . . but still, he pauses. It would be inhuman to leave it out there in the cold, he thinks (not that it is much warmer in here; in spite of the battery-powered heater, he can see the cold cloud of his breath)—but still he hesitates. A cold finger of fear is probing just below his heart. This has been a bad season in Tarker's Mills; there have been omens of evil on the land. Arnie has his father's Welsh blood strong in his veins, and he doesn't like the feel of things.

Before he can decide what to do about his visitor, the low-pitched whining rises to a snarl. There is a thud as something incredibly heavy hits the door . . . draws back . . . hits again. The door trembles in its frame, and a puff of snow billows in from the top.

Arnie Westrum stares around, looking for something to shore it up with, but before he can do more than reach for the flimsy

13

chair he has been sitting in, the snarling thing strikes the door again with incredible force, splintering it from top to bottom.

It holds for a moment longer, bowed in on a vertical line, and lodged in it, kicking and lunging, its snout wrinkled back in a snarl, its yellow eyes blazing, is the biggest wolf Arnie has ever seen...

And its snarls sound terribly like human words.

The door splinters, groans, gives. In a moment the thing will be inside.

In the corner, amongst a welter of tools, a pick leans against the wall. Arnie lunges for it and seizes it as the wolf thrusts its way inside and crouches, its yellow eyes gleaming at the cornered man. Its ears are flattened back, furry triangles. Its tongue lolls. Behind it, snow gusts in through a door that has been shattered down the center.

It springs with a snarl, and Arnie Westrum swings the pick.

Once.

Outside, the feeble lamplight shines raggedly on the snow through the splintered door.

The wind whoops and howls.

The screams begin.

Something inhuman has come to Tarker's Mills, as unseen as the full moon riding the night sky high above. It is the Werewolf, and there is no more reason for its coming now than there would be for the arrival of cancer, or a psychotic with murder on his mind, or a killer tornado. Its time is now, its place is here, in this little Maine town where baked bean church suppers are a weekly event, where small boys and girls still bring apples to their teachers, where the Nature Outings of the Senior Citizens' Club are religiously reported in the weekly paper. Next week there will be news of a darker variety.

Outside, its tracks begin to fill up with snow, and the shriek

of the wind seems savage with pleasure. There is nothing of God or Light in that heartless sound—it is all black winter and dark ice.

The cycle of the Werewolf has begun.

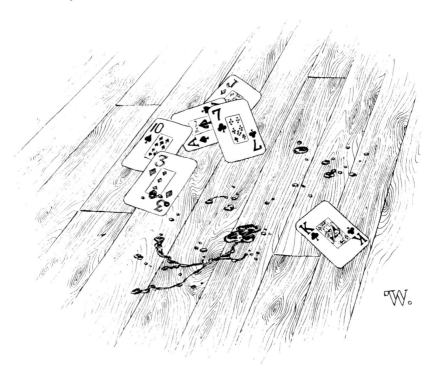

JANUARY

FEBRUARY

MARCH

APRIL

MAY

JUNE

JULY

AUGUST

SEPTEMBER

OCTOBER

NOVEMBER

DECEMBER

Love, Stella Randolph thinks, lying in her narrow virgin's bed, and through her window streams the cold blue light of a St. Valentine's Day full moon.

Oh love love love, love would be like—

This year Stella Randolph, who runs the Tarker's Mills Set 'n Sew, has received twenty Valentines—one from Paul Newman, one from Robert Redford, one from John Travolta...even one from Ace Frehley of the rock group Kiss. They stand open on the bureau across the room from her, illuminated in the moon's cold blue light. She sent them all to herself, this year as every year.

Love would be like a kiss at dawn...or the last kiss, the real one, at the end of the Harlequin romance stories...love would be like roses in twilight...

They laugh at her in Tarker's Mills, yes, you bet. Small boys joke and snigger at her from behind their hands (and sometimes, if they are safe across the street and Constable Neary isn't around, they will chant *Fatty-Fatty-Two-By-Four* in their sweet, high mocking sopranos), but she knows about love, and about the moon. Her store is failing by inches, and she weighs too much, but now, on this night of dreams with the moon a bitter blue flood through frost-traced windows, it seems to her that love is still a possibility, love and the scent of summer as *he* comes...

Love would be like the rough feel of a man's cheek, that rub and scratch—

And suddenly there is a scratching at the window.

She starts up on her elbows, the coverlet falling away from her ample bosom. The moonlight has been blocked out by a dark shape—amorphous but clearly masculine, and she thinks: *I am dreaming...and in my dreams, I will let him come...in my dreams I will let myself come. They use the word dirty, but the word is clean, the word is right; love would be like coming.*

She rises, convinced that this is a dream, because there *is* a man crouched out there, a man she *knows*, a man she passes on the street nearly everyday. It is—

(love love is coming, love has come)

But as her pudgy fingers fall on the cold sash of the window she sees it is not a man at all; it is an animal out there, a huge, shaggy wolf, his forepaws on the outer sill, his rear legs buried up to the haunches in the snowdrift which crouches against the west side of her house, here on the outskirts of town.

But it's Valentine's day and there will be love, she thinks; her eyes have deceived her even in her dream. It is a man, *that* man, and he is so wickedly handsome.

(wickedness yes love would be like wickedness)

and he has come this moon-decked night and he will take her. He will—

She throws the window up and it is the blast of cold air billowing her filmy blue nightgown out behind that tells her that *this is no dream.* The man is gone and with a sensation like swooning she realizes he was never there. She takes a shuddering, groping step backward and the wolf leaps smoothly into her room and shakes itself, spraying a dreamy sugarpuff of snow in the darkness.

But love! Love is like . . . is like . . . like a scream—

Too late she remembers Arnie Westrum, torn apart in the railroad shack to the west of town only a month before. Too late . . .

The wolf pads toward her, yellow eyes gleaming with cool lust. Stella Randolph backs slowly toward her narrow virgin's bed until the back of her pudgy knees strike the frame and she collapses upon it.

Moonlight parts the beast's shaggy fur in a silvery streak.

On the bureau the Valentine cards shiver minutely in the

breeze from the open window; one of them falls and seesaws lazily to the floor, cutting the air in big silent arcs.

The wolf puts its paw up on the bed, one on either side of her, and she can smell its breath...hot, but somehow not unpleasant. Its yellow eyes stare into her.

"Lover," she whispers, and closes her eyes.

It falls upon her.

Love is like dying.

JANUARY
FEBRUARY
MARCH
APRIL
MAY
JUNE
JULY
AUGUST
SEPTEMBER
OCTOBER
NOVEMBER
DECEMBER

The last real blizzard of the year—heavy, wet snow turning to sleet as dusk comes on and the night closes in—has brought branches tumbling down all over Tarker's Mills with the heavy gunshot cracks of rotted wood. Mother Nature's pruning out her deadwood, Milt Sturmfuller, the town librarian, tells his wife over coffee. He is a thin man with a narrow head and pale blue eyes, and he has kept his pretty, silent wife in a bondage of terror for twelve years now. There are a few who suspect the truth—Constable Neary's wife Joan is one—but the town can be a dark place, and no one knows for sure but them. The town keeps its secrets.

Milt likes his phrase so well that he says it again: Yep, Mother Nature is pruning her deadwood . . . and then the lights go out and Donna Lee Sturmfuller utters a gasping little scream. She also spills her coffee.

You clean that up, her husband says coldly. You clean that up right . . . now.

Yes, honey. Okay.

In the dark, she fumbles for a dishtowel with which to clean up the spilled coffee and barks her shin on a footstool. She cries out. In the dark, her husband laughs heartily. He finds his wife's pain more amusing than anything, except maybe the jokes they have in The Reader's Digest. Those jokes—Humor in Uniform, Life in These United States—really tickle his funny-bone.

As well as deadwood, Mother Nature has pruned a few pow-erlines out by Tarker Brook this wild March night; the sleet has coated the big lines, growing heavier and heavier, until they have parted and fallen on the road like a nest of snakes, lazily turning and spitting blue fire.

All of Tarker's Mills goes dark.

As if finally satisfied, the storm begins to slack off, and not long before midnight the temperature has plummeted from thirty-three degrees to sixteen. Slush freezes solid in weird sculptures. Old Man Hague's hayfield—known locally as Forty

Acre Field—takes on a cracked glaze look. The houses remain dark; oil furnaces tick and cool. No linesman is yet able to get up the skating-rink roads.

The clouds pull apart. A full moon slips in and out between the remnants. The ice coating Main Street glows like dead bone.

In the night, something begins to howl.

Later, no one will be able to say where the sound came from; it was everywhere and nowhere as the full moon painted the darkened houses of the village, everywhere and nowhere as the March wind began to rise and moan like a dead Berserker winding his horn, it drifted on the wind, lonely and savage.

Donna Lee hears it as her unpleasant husband sleeps the sleep of the just beside her; constable Neary hears it as he stands at the bedroom window of his Laurel Street apartment in his longhandles; Ollie Parker, the fat and ineffectual grammar school principal hears it in his own bedroom; others hear it, as well. One of them is a boy in a wheelchair.

No one sees it. And no one knows the name of the drifter the linesman found the next morning when he finally got out by Tarker Brook to repair the downed cables. The drifter was coated with ice, head cocked back in a silent scream, ragged old coat and shirt beneath chewed open. The drifter sat in a frozen pool of his own blood, staring at the downed lines, his hands still held up in a warding-off gesture with ice between the fingers.

And all around him are pawprints.

Wolfprints.

W.

31

JANUARY
FEBRUARY
MARCH
APRIL
MAY
JUNE
JULY
AUGUST
SEPTEMBER
OCTOBER
NOVEMBER
DECEMBER

APRIL

WRIGHTSON 1981

By the middle of the month, the last of the snow flurries have turned to showers of rain and something amazing is happening in Tarker's Mills: it is starting to green up. The ice in Matty Tellingham's cow-pond has gone out, and the patches of snow in the tract of forest called the Big Woods have all begun to shrink. It seems that the old and wonderful trick is going to happen again. Spring is going to come.

The townsfolk celebrate it in small ways in spite of the shadow that has fallen over the town. Gramma Hague bakes pies and sets them out on the kitchen windowsill to cool. On Sunday, at the Grace Baptist Church, the Reverend Lester Lowe reads from The Song of Solomon and preaches a sermon titled "The Spring of the Lord's Love." On a more secular note, Chris Wrightson, the biggest drunk in Tarker's Mills, throws his Great Spring Drunk and staggers off in the silvery, unreal light of a nearly full April moon. Billy Robertson, bartender and proprietor of the pub, Tarker's Mills' only saloon, watches him go and mutters to the barmaid, "If that wolf takes someone tonight, I guess it'll be Chris."

"Don't talk about it," the barmaid replies, shuddering. Her name is Elise Fournier, she is twenty-four, and she attends the Grace Baptist and sings in the choir because she has a crush on the Rev. Lowe. But she plans to leave the Mills by summer; crush or no crush, this wolf business has begun to scare her. She has begun to think that the tips might be better in Portsmouth . . . and the only wolves there wore sailors' uniforms.

Nights in Tarker's Mills as the moon grows fat for the third time that year are uncomfortable times . . . the days are better. On the town common, there is suddenly a skyful of kites each afternoon.

Brady Kincaid, eleven years old, has gotten a Vulture for his birthday and has lost all track of time in his pleasure at feeling the kite tug in his hands like a live thing, watching it dip and swoop through the blue sky above the bandstand. He has forgotten about going home for supper, he is unaware that the other kite-fliers have left one by one, with their box-kites and tent-kites and Aluminum Fliers tucked securely under their arms, unaware that he is alone.

It is the fading daylight and advancing blue shadows which finally make him realize he has lingered too long—that, and the moon just rising over the woods at the edge of the park. For the first time it is a warm-weather moon, bloated and orange instead of a cold white, but Brady doesn't notice this; he is only aware that he has stayed too long, his father is probably going to whup him . . . and dark is coming.

At school, he has laughed at his schoolmates' fanciful tales of the werewolf they say killed the drifter last month, Stella Randolph the month before, Arnie Westrum the month before that. But he doesn't laugh now. As the moon turns April dusk into a bloody furnace-glow, the stories seem all too real.

He begins to wind twine onto his ball as fast as he can, dragging the Vulture with its two bloodshot eyes out of the darkening sky. He brings it in too fast, and the breeze suddenly dies. As a result, the kite dives behind the bandstand.

He starts toward it, winding up string as he goes, glancing nervously back over his shoulder . . . and suddenly the string begins to twitch and move in his hands, sawing back and forth. It reminds him of the way his fishing pole feels when he's hooked a big one in Tarker's Stream, above the Mills. He looks at it, frowning, and the line goes slack.

A shattering roar suddenly fills the night and Brady Kincaid screams. He believes *now*, Yes, he believes *now*, all right, but it's too late and his scream is lost under that snarling roar that rises in a sudden, chilling glissade to a howl.

The wolf is running toward him, running on two legs, its shaggy pelt painted orange with moonfire, its eyes glaring green lamps, and in one paw—a paw with human fingers and claws where the nails should be—is Brady's Vulture kite. It is fluttering madly.

Brady turns to run and dry arms suddenly encircle him; he can smell something like blood and cinnamon, and he is found the next day propped against the War Memorial, headless and disembowelled, the Vulture kite in one stiffening hand.

The kite flutters, as if trying for the sky, as the search-party turn away, horrified and sick. It flutters because the breeze has already come up. It flutters as if it knows this will be a good day for kites.

JANUARY
FEBRUARY
MARCH
APRIL
MAY
JUNE
JULY
AUGUST
SEPTEMBER
OCTOBER
NOVEMBER
DECEMBER

On the night before Homecoming Sunday at the Grace Baptist Church, the Reverend Lester Lowe has a terrible dream from which he awakes, trembling, bathed in sweat, staring at the narrow windows of the parsonage. Through them, across the road, he can see his church. Moonlight falls through the parsonage's bedroom windows in still silver beams, and for one moment he fully expects to see the werewolf the old codgers have all been whispering about. Then he closes his eyes, begging for forgiveness for his superstitious lapse, finishing his prayer by whispering the "For Jesus' sake, amen"—so his mother taught him to end all his prayers.

Ah, but the dream...

In his dream it was tomorrow and he had been preaching the Homecoming Sermon. The church is always filled on Homecoming Sunday (only the oldest of the old codgers still call it Old Home Sunday now), and instead of looking out on pews half or wholly empty as he does on most Sundays, every bench is full.

In his dream he has been preaching with a fire and a force that he rarely attains in reality (he tends to drone, which may be one reason that Grace Baptist's attendance has fallen off so drastically in the last ten years or so). This morning his tongue seems to have been touched with the Pentecostal Fire, and he realizes that he is preaching the greatest sermon of his life, and its subject is this: THE BEAST WALKS AMONG US. Over and over he hammers at the point, vaguely aware that his voice has grown roughly strong, that his words have attained an almost poetic rhythm.

The Beast, he tells them, is everywhere. The Great Satan, he tells them, can be anywhere. At a high school dance. Buying a deck of Marlboros and a Bic butane lighter down at the Trading Post. Standing in front of Brighton's Drug, eating a Slim Jim, and waiting for the 4:40 Greyhound from Bangor to pull in. The Beast might be sitting next to you at a band concert or having a piece of pie at the Chat 'n Chew on Main Street. The Beast, he tells them, his voice dropping to a whisper that throbs, and no eye wanders. He has them in thrall. Watch for the Beast, for he may smile and say he is your neighbor, but oh my brethren, his teeth are sharp and you may mark the uneasy way in which his eyes roll. He is the Beast, and he is here, now, in Tarker's Mills. He—

But here he breaks off, his eloquence gone, because something terrible is happening out there in his sunny church. His congregation is beginning to change, and he realizes with horror that they are turning into werewolves, all of them, all three hundred of them: Victor Bowle, the head selectman, usually so white and fat and pudgy . . . his skin is turning brown, roughening, darkening with hair! Violet MacKenzie, who teaches piano . . . her narrow spinster's body is filling out, her thin nose flattening and splaying! The fat science teacher, Elbert Freeman, seems to be growing fatter, his shiny blue suit is splitting, clocksprings of hair are bursting out like the stuffing from an old sofa! His fat lips split back like bladders to reveal teeth the size of piano keys!

The Beast, the Rev. Lowe tries to say in his dreams, but the words fail him and he stumbles back from the pulpit in horror as Cal Blodwin, the Grace Baptist's head deacon, shambles down the center aisle, snarling, money spilling from the silver collection plate, his head cocked to one side. Violet MacKenzie leaps on him and they roll in the aisle together, biting and shrieking in voices which are almost human.

And now the others join in and the sound is like the zoo at feeding-time, and this time the Rev. Lowe *screams* it out, in a kind of ecstasy: *"The Beast! The Beast is everywhere! Everywhere! Every—"* But his voice is no longer his voice; it has become an inarticulate snarling sound, and when he looks down, he sees the hands protruding from the sleeves of his good black suitcoat have become snaggled paws.

And then he awakes.

Only a dream, he thinks, lying back down again. *Only a dream, thank God.*

But when he opens the church doors that morning, the morning of Homecoming Sunday, the morning after the full moon, it is no dream he sees; it is the gutted body of Clyde Corliss, who has done janitorial work for years, hanging face-down over the pulpit. His push-broom leans close by.

None of this is a dream; the Rev. Lowe only wishes it could be. He opens his mouth, hitches in a great, gasping breath, and begins to scream.

Spring has come back again—and this year, the Beast has come with it.

JANUARY
FEBRUARY
MARCH
APRIL
MAY
JUNE
JULY
AUGUST
SEPTEMBER
OCTOBER
NOVEMBER
DECEMBER

JUNE

On the shortest night of the year, Alfie Knopfler, who runs the Chat 'n Chew, Tarker's Mills' only cafe, polishes his long Formica counter to a gleaming brightness, the sleeves of his white shirt rolled to past his muscular, tattooed elbows. The cafe is for the moment completely empty, and as he finishes with the counter, he pauses for a moment, looking out into the street, thinking that he lost his virginity on a fragrant early summer night like this one—the girl had been Arlene McCune, who is now Arlene Bessey, and married to one of Bangor's most successful young lawyers. God, how she had moved that night on the back seat of his car, and how sweet the night had smelled!

The door into summer swings open and lets in a bright tide of moonlight. He supposes the cafe is deserted because the Beast is supposed to walk when the moon in full, but Alfie is neither scared nor worried; not scared because he weighs two-twenty and most of it is still good old Navy muscle, not worried because he knows the regulars will be in bright and early to-morrow morning for their eggs and their homefries and coffee. Maybe, he thinks, I'll close her up a little early tonight—shut off the coffee urn, button her up, get a six-pack down at the Market Basket, and take in the second picture at the drive-in. June, June, full moon—a good night for the drive-in and a few beers. A good night to remember the conquests of the past.

He is turning toward the coffee-maker when the door opens, and he turns back, resigned.

"Say! How you doin'?" he asks, because the customer is one of his regulars . . . although he rarely sees this customer later than ten in the morning.

The customer nods, and the two of them pass a few friendly words.

"Coffee?" Alfie asks, as the customer slips onto one of the padded red counter-stools.

"Please."

Well, still time to catch that second show, Alfie thinks, turning to the coffee-maker. He don't look like he's good for long. Tired. Sick, maybe. Still plenty of time to—

Shock wipes out the rest of his thought. Alfie gapes stupidly. The coffee-maker is as spotless as everything else in the Chat 'n Chew, the stainless steel cylinder bright as a metal mirror. And in its smoothly bulging convex surface he sees something as unbelievable as it is hideous. His customer, someone he sees every day, someone *everyone* in Tarker's Mills sees every day, is changing. The customer's face is somehow shifting, melting, thickening, broadening. The customer's cotton shirt is stretching, stretching... and suddenly the shirt's seams begin to pull apart, and absurdly, all Alfie Knopfler can think of is that show his little nephew Ray used to like to watch, *The Incredible Hulk*.

The customer's pleasant, unremarkable face is becoming something bestial. The customer's mild brown eyes have lightened; have become a terrible gold-green. The customer screams ... but the scream breaks apart, drops like an elevator through registers of sound, and becomes a bellowing growl of rage.

It—the thing, the Beast, werewolf, whatever it is—gropes at the smooth Formica and knocks over a sugar-shaker. It grabs the thick glass cylinder as it rolls, spraying sugar, and heaves it at the wall where the specials are taped up, still bellowing.

Alfie wheels around and his hip knocks the coffee urn off the shelf. It hits the floor with a bang and sprays hot coffee everywhere, burning his ankles. He cries out in pain and fear. Yes, he is afraid now, his two hundred and twenty pounds of good Navy muscle are forgotten now, his nephew Ray is forgotten now, his back seat coupling with Arlene McCune is forgotten now, and there is only the Beast, here now like some horror-monster in a drive-in movie, a horror-monster that has come right out of the screen.

It leaps on top of the counter with a terrible muscular ease, its slacks in tatters, its shirt in rags. Alfie can hear keys and change jingling in its pockets.

It leaps at Alfie, and Alfie tries to dodge, but he trips over the coffee urn and goes sprawling on the red linoleum. There is another shattering roar, a flood of warm yellow breath, and then a great red pain as the creature's jaws sink into the deltoid muscles of his back and rip upward with terrifying force. Blood sprays the floor, the counter, the grille.

Alfie staggers to his feet with a huge, ragged, spraying hole in his back; he is trying to scream, and white moonlight, summer moonlight, floods in through the windows and dazzles his eyes.

The Beast leaps on him again.

Moonlight is the last thing Alfie sees.

JANUARY
FEBRUARY
MARCH
APRIL
MAY
JUNE
JULY
AUGUST
SEPTEMBER
OCTOBER
NOVEMBER
DECEMBER

They cancelled the Fourth of July.

Marty Coslaw gets remarkably little sympathy from the people closest to him when he tells them that. Perhaps it is because they simply don't understand the depth of his pain.

"Don't be foolish," his mother tells him brusquely—she is often brusque with him, and when she has to rationalize this brusqueness to herself, she tells herself she will not spoil the boy just because he is handicapped, because he is going to spend his life sitting in a wheelchair.

"Wait until next year!" his dad tells him, clapping him on the back. "Twice as good! Twice as doodly-damn good! You'll see, little bitty buddy! Hey, hey!"

Herman Coslaw is the phys ed teacher at the Tarker's Mills grammar school, and he almost always talks to his son in what Marty thinks of as dad's Big Pal voice. He also says "Hey, hey!" a great deal. The truth is, Marty makes Herman Coslaw a little nervous. Herman lives in a world of violently active children, kids who run races, bash baseballs, swim rally sprints. And in the midst of directing all this he would sometimes look up and see Marty, somewhere close by, sitting in his wheelchair, watching. It made Herman nervous, and when he was nervous, he spoke in his bellowing Big Pal voice, and said "Hey, hey!" or "doodly-damn" and called Marty his "little bitty buddy."

"Ha-ha, so you finally didn't get something you wanted!" his big sister says when he tries to tell her how he had looked forward to this night, how he looks forward to it every year, the flowers of light in the sky over the Commons, the flashgun pops of brightness followed by the thudding *KER-WHAMP!* sounds that roll back and forth between the low hills that surrounded the town. Kate is thirteen to Marty's ten, and convinced that everyone loves Marty just because he can't walk. She is delighted that the fireworks have been cancelled.

Even Grandfather Coslaw, who could usually be counted on for sympathy, hadn't been impressed. "Nobody is cancellin der fort of Choo-lie, boy," he said in his heavy Slavic accent. He

61

was sitting on the verandah, and Marty buzzed out through the french doors in his battery-powered wheelchair to talk to him. Grandfather Coslaw sat looking down the slope of the lawn toward the woods, a glass of schnapps in one hand. This had happened on July 2, two days ago. "It's just the fireworks they cancel. And you know why."

Marty did. The killer, that was why. In the papers now they were calling him The Full Moon Killer, but Marty had heard plenty of whispers around school before classes had ended for the summer. Lots of kids were saying that The Full Moon Killer wasn't a real man at all, but some sort of supernatural creature. A werewolf, maybe. Marty didn't believe that—werewolves were strictly for the horror movies—but he supposed there could be some kind of crazy guy out there who only felt the urge to kill when the moon was full. The fireworks have been cancelled because of their dirty rotten *curfew.*

In January, sitting in his wheelchair by the french doors and looking out onto the verandah, watching the wind blow bitter veils of snow across the frozen crust, or standing by the front door, stiff as a statue in his locked leg-braces, watching the other kids pull their sleds toward Wright's Hill, just *thinking* of the fireworks made a difference. Thinking of a warm summer night, a cold Coke, of fire-roses blooming in the dark, and pinwheels, and an American flag made of Roman candles.

But now they have cancelled the fireworks . . . and no matter what anyone says, Marty feels that it is really the Fourth *itself*— *his* Fourth—that they have done to death.

Only his Uncle Al, who blew into town late this morning to have the traditional salmon and fresh peas with the family, had understood. He had listened closely, standing on the verandah tiles in his dripping bathing suit (the others were swimming and laughing in the Coslaws' new pool on the other side of the house) after lunch.

Marty finished and looked at Uncle Al anxiously.

"Do you see what I mean? Do you get it? It hasn't got anything to do with being crippled, like Katie says, or getting the fireworks all mixed up with America, like Granpa thinks. It's just not right, when you look forward to something for so long . . . it's not right for Victor Bowle and some dumb town *council* to come along and take it away. Not when it's something you really need. Do you get it?"

There was a long, agonizing pause while Uncle Al considered Marty's question. Time enough for Marty to hear the kick-rattle of the diving board at the deep end of the pool, followed by Dad's hearty bellow: "Lookin' good, Kate! Hey, hey! Lookin' *reeeeeel . . . good!*"

Then Uncle Al said quietly: "Sure I get it. And I got something for you, I think. Maybe you can make your own Fourth."

"My own Fourth? What do you mean?"

"Come on out to my car, Marty. I've got something . . . well, I'll show you." And he was striding away along the concrete path that circled the house before Marty could ask him what he meant.

His wheelchair hummed along the path to the driveway, away from the sounds of the pool—splashes, laughing screams, the *kathummmm* of the diving board. Away from his father's booming Big Pal voice. The sound of his wheelchair was a low, steady hum that Marty barely heard—all his life that sound, and the clank of his braces, had been the music of his movement.

Uncle Al's car was a low-slung Mercedes convertible. Marty knew his parents disapproved of it ("Twenty-eight-thousand-dollar deathtrap," his mother had once called it with a brusque little sniff), but Marty loved it. Once Uncle Al had taken him for a ride on some of the back roads that crisscrossed Tarker's Mills, and he had driven fast—seventy, maybe eighty. He wouldn't tell Marty how fast they were going. "If you don't know, you won't be scared," he had said. But Marty hadn't

63

been scared. His belly had been sore the next day from laughing.

Uncle Al took something out of the glove-compartment of his car, and as Marty rolled up and stopped, he put a bulky cellophane package on the boy's withered thighs. "Here you go, kid," he said. "Happy Fourth of July."

The first thing Marty saw were exotic Chinese markings on the package's label. Then he saw what was inside, and his heart seemed to squeeze up in his chest. The cellophane package was full of fireworks.

"The ones that look like pyramids are Twizzers," Uncle Al said.

Marty, absolutely stunned with joy, moved his lips to speak, but nothing came out.

"Light the fuses, set them down, and they spray as many colors as there are on a dragon's breath. The tubes with the thin sticks coming out of them are bottle-rockets. Put them in an empty Coke bottle and up they go. The little ones are fountains. There are two Roman candles . . . and of course, a package of firecrackers. But you better set those off tomorrow."

Uncle Al cast an eye toward the noises coming from the pool.

"Thank you!" Marty was finally able to gasp. "Thank you, Uncle Al!"

"Just keep mum about where you got them," Uncle Al said. "A nod's as good as a wink to a blind horse, right?"

"Right, right," Marty babbled, although he had no idea what nods, winks, and blind horses had to do with fireworks. "But are you sure you don't want them, Uncle Al?"

"I can get more," Uncle Al said. "I know a guy over in Bridgton. He'll be doing business until it gets dark." He put a hand on Marty's head. "You keep your Fourth after everyone else goes to bed. Don't shoot off any of the noisy ones and wake them all up. And for Christ's sake don't blow your hand off, or my big sis will never speak to me again."

Then Uncle Al laughed and climbed into his car and roared the engine into life. He raised his hand in a half-salute to Marty and then was gone while Marty was still trying to stutter his thanks. He sat there for a moment looking after his uncle, swallowing hard to keep from crying. Then he put the packet of fireworks into his shirt and buzzed back to the house and his room. In his mind he was already waiting for night to come and everyone to be asleep.

He is the first one in bed that night. His mother comes in and kisses him goodnight (brusquely, not looking at his stick-like legs under the sheet). "You okay, Marty?"

"Yes, mom."

She pauses, as if to say something more, and then gives her head a little shake. She leaves.

His sister Kate comes in. She doesn't kiss him; merely leans her head close to his neck so he can smell the chlorine in her hair and she whispers: "See? you don't always get what you want just because you're a cripple."

"You might be surprised what I get," he says softly, and she regards him for a moment with narrow suspicion before going out.

His father comes in last and sits on the side of Marty's bed. He speaks in his booming Big Pal voice. "Everything okay, big guy? You're off to bed early. *Real* early."

"Just feeling a little tired, daddy."

"Okay." He slaps one of Marty's wasted legs with his big hand, winces unconsciously, and then gets up in a hurry. "Sorry about the fireworks, but just wait till next year! Hey, hey! Rootie-patootie!"

Marty smiles a small, secret smile.

So then he begins the waiting for the rest of the house to go to bed. It takes a long time. The TV runs on and on in the living room, the canned laughtracks often augmented by Katie's shrill giggles. The toilet in Granpa's bedroom goes with a bang and a flush. His mother chats on the phone, wishes someone a happy Fourth, says yes, it was a shame the fireworks show had been cancelled, but she thought that, under the circumstances, everyone understood why it had to be. Yes, Marty had been disappointed. Once, near the end of her conversation, she laughs, and when she laughs, she doesn't sound a bit brusque. She hardly ever laughs around Marty.

Every now and then, as seven-thirty became eight and nine, his hand creeps under his pillow to make sure the cellophane bag of fireworks is still there. Around nine-thirty, when the moon gets high enough to peer into his window and flood his room with silvery light, the house finally begins to wind down.

The TV clicks off. Katie goes to bed, protesting that all her friends got to stay up *late* in the summer. After she's gone, Marty's folks sit in the parlor awhile longer, their conversation only murmurs. And...

...and maybe he slept, because when he next touches the wonderful bag of fireworks, he realizes that the house is totally still and the moon has become even brighter—bright enough to cast shadows. He takes the bag out along with the book of matches he found earlier. He tucks his pajama shirt into his pajama pants; drops both the bag and the matches into his shirt, and prepares to get out of bed.

This is an operation for Marty, but not a painful one, as people sometimes seemed to think. There is no feeling of any kind in his legs, so there can be no pain. He grips the headboard of the bed, pulls himself up to a sitting position, and then shifts his legs over the edge of the bed one by one. He does this one-handed, using his other hand to hold the rail which begins at his bed and runs all the way around the room. Once he had tried moving his legs with both hands and somersaulted help-

lessly head over heels onto the floor. The crash brought everyone running. "You stupid show-off!" Kate had whispered fiercely into his ear after he had been helped into his chair, a little shaken up but laughing crazily in spite of the swelling on one temple and his split lip. "You want to kill yourself? Huh?" And then she had run out of the room, crying.

Once he's sitting on the edge of the bed, he wipes his hands on the front of his shirt to make sure they're dry and won't slip. Then he uses the rail to go hand over hand to his wheelchair. His useless scarecrow legs, so much dead weight, drag along behind him. The moonlight is bright enough to cast his shadow, bright and crisp, on the floor ahead of him.

His wheelchair is on the brake, and he swings into it with confident ease. He pauses for a moment, catching his breath, listening to the silence of the house. *Don't shoot off any of the noisy ones tonight,* Uncle Al had said, and listening to the silence, Marty knows that was right. He will keep his Fourth by himself and to himself and no one will know. At least not until tomorrow when they see the blackened husks of the twizzers and the fountains out on the verandah, and then it wouldn't matter. *As many colors as there are on a dragon's breath,* Uncle Al had said. But Marty supposes there's no law against a dragon breathing silently.

He lets the brake off his chair and flips the power switch. The little amber eye, the one that means his battery is well-charged, comes on in the dark. Marty pushes RIGHT TURN. The chair rotates right. Hey, hey. When it is facing the verandah doors, he pushes FORWARD. The chair rolls forward, humming quietly.

Marty slips the latch on the double doors, pushes FORWARD again, and rolls outside. He tears open the wonderful bag of fireworks and then pauses for a moment, captivated by the summer night—the somnolent chirr of the crickets, the low, fragrant breeze that barely stirs the leaves of the trees at the edge of the woods, the almost unearthly radiance of the moon.

He can wait no longer. He brings out a snake, strikes a match, lights its fuse, and watches in entranced silence as it splutters green-blue fire and grows magically, writhing and spitting flame from its tail.

The Fourth, he thinks, his eyes alight. *The Fourth, the Fourth, happy Fourth of July to me!*

The snake's bright flame gutters low, flickers, goes out. Marty lights one of the triangular twizzers and watches as it spouts fire as yellow as his dad's lucky golf shirt. Before it can go out, he lights a second that shoots off light as dusky-red as the roses which grow beside the picket fence around the new pool. Now a wonderful smell of spent powder fills the night for the wind to rafter and pull slowly away.

His groping hands pull out the flat packet of firecrackers next, and he has opened them before he realizes that to light these would be calamity—their jumping, snapping, machine-gun roar would wake the whole neighborhood: fire, flood, alarm, excursion. All of those, and one ten-year-old boy named Martin Coslaw in the doghouse until Christmas, most likely.

He pushes the Black Cats further up on his lap, gropes happily in the bag again, and comes out with the biggest twizzer of all—a World Class Twizzer if ever there was one. It is almost as big as his closed fist. He lights it with mixed fright and delight, and tosses it.

Red light as bright as hellfire fills the night...and it is by this shifting, feverish glow that Marty sees the bushes at the fringe of the woods below the verandah shake and part. There is a low noise, half-cough, half-snarl. The Beast appears.

It stands for a moment at the base of the lawn and seems to scent the air...and then it begins to shamble up the slope toward where Marty sits on the slate flagstones in his wheelchair, his eyes bulging, his upper body shrinking against the canvas back of his chair. The Beast is hunched over, but it is clearly walking on its two rear legs. Walking the way a man would walk. The red light of the twizzer skates hellishly across its green eyes.

It moves slowly, its wide nostrils flaring rhythmically. Scenting prey, almost surely scenting that prey's weakness. Marty can *smell* it—its hair, its sweat, its savagery. It grunts again. Its thick upper lip, the color of liver, wrinkles back to show its heavy tusk-like teeth. Its pelt is painted a dull silvery-red.

It has almost reached him—its clawed hands, so like-unlike human hands, reaching for his throat—when the boy remembers the packet of firecrackers. Hardly aware he is going to do it, he strikes a match and touches it to the master fuse. The fuse spits a hot line of red sparks that singe the fine hair on the back of his hand, crisping them. The werewolf, momentarily offbalance, draws backwards, uttering a questioning grunt that, like his hands, is nearly human. Marty throws the packet of firecrackers in its face.

They go off in a banging, flashing train of light and sound. The beast utters a screech-roar of pain and rage; it staggers backwards, clawing at the explosions that tattoo grains of fire and burning gunpowder into its face. Marty sees one of its lamplike green eyes whiff out as four crackers go off at once with a terrific thundering KA-POW! at the side of its muzzle. Now its screams are pure agony. It claws at its face, bellowing, and as the first lights go on in the Coslaw house it turns and bounds back down the lawn toward the woods, leaving behind it only a smell of singed fur and the first frightened and bewildered cries from the house.

"What was that?" His mother's voice, not sounding a bit brusque.

"Who's there, goddammit?" His father, not sounding very much like a Big Pal.

"Marty?" Kate, her voice quavering, not sounding mean at all. "Marty, are you all right?"

Grandfather Coslaw sleeps through the whole thing.

Marty leans back in his wheelchair as the big red twizzer gutters its way to extinction. Its light is now the mild and lovely pink of an early sunrise. He is too shocked to weep. But his shock is not entirely a dark emotion, although the next day his parents will bundle him off to visit his Uncle Jim and Aunt Ida over in Stowe, Vermont, where he will stay until the end of summer vacation (the police concur; they feel that The Full Moon Killer might try to attack Marty again, and silence him). There is a deep exultation in him. It is stronger than the shock. He has looked into the terrible face of the Beast and lived. And there is simple, childlike joy in him, as well, a quiet joy he will never be able to communicate later to anyone, not even Uncle Al, who might have understood. He feels this joy because the fireworks have happened after all.

And while his parents stewed and wondered about his psyche, and if he would have complexes from the experience, Marty Coslaw came to believe in his heart that it had been the best Fourth of all.

JANUARY
FEBRUARY
MARCH
APRIL
MAY
JUNE
JULY
AUGUST
SEPTEMBER
OCTOBER
NOVEMBER
DECEMBER

AUGUST

"Sure, I think it's a werewolf," Constable Neary says. He speaks too loudly—maybe accidentally, more like accidentally on purpose—and all conversation in Stan's Barber Shop comes to a halt. It is going on just half-past August, the hottest August anyone can remember in Tarker's Mills for years, and tonight the moon will be just one day past full. So the town holds its breath, waiting.

Constable Neary surveys his audience and then goes on from his place in Stan Pelky's middle barber chair, speaking weightily, speaking judicially, speaking psychologically, all from the depths of his high school education (Neary is a big, beefy man, and in high school he mostly made touchdowns for the Tarker's Mills Tigers; his classwork earned him some C's and not a few D's).

"There are guys," he tells them, "who are kind of like two people. Kind of like split personalities, you know. They are what I'd call fucking schizos."

He pauses to appreciate the respectful silence which greets this and then goes on:

"Now this guy, I think he's like that. I don't think he knows what he's doing when the moon gets full and he goes out and kills somebody. He could be anybody—a teller at the bank, a gas-jockey at one of those stations out on the Town Road, maybe even someone right here now. In the sense of being an animal inside and looking perfectly normal outside, yeah, you bet. But if you mean, do I think there's a guy who sprouts hair and howls at the moon . . . no. That shit's for kids."

"What about the Coslaw boy, Neary?" Stan asks, continuing to work carefully around the roll of fat at the base of Neary's neck. His long, sharp scissors go *snip . . . snip . . . snip.*

"Just proves what I said," Neary responds with some exasperation. "That shit's for kids."

In truth, he *feels* exasperated about what's happened with Marty Coslaw. Here, in this boy, is the first eyeball witness to the freak that's killed six people in his town, including Neary's good friend Alfie Knopfler. And is he allowed to interview the boy? No. Does he even know where the boy is? No! He's had to make do with a deposition furnished to him by the State Police, and he had to bow and scrape and just-a-damn-bout *beg* to get that much. All because he's a small-town constable, what the State Police think of as a kiddie-cop, not able to tie his own shoes. All because he doesn't have one of their numbfuck Smokey Bear hats. And the deposition! He might as well have used it to wipe his ass with. According to the Coslaw kid, this "beast" stood about seven feet tall, was naked, was covered with dark hair all over his body. He had big teeth and green eyes and smelled like a load of panther-shit. He had claws, but the claws looked like hands. He thought it had a tail. *A tail,* for Chrissake.

"Maybe," Kenny Franklin says from his place in the row of chairs along the wall, "maybe it's some kind of disguise this fella puts on. Like a mask and all, you know."

"I don't believe it," Neary says emphatically, and nods his head to emphasize the point. Stan has to draw his scissors back in a hurry to avoid putting one of the blades into that beefy roll of fat at the back of Neary's neck. "Nossir! I don't believe it! Kid heard a lot of these werewolf stories at school before it closed for the summer—he admitted as much—and then he didn't have nothing to do but sit there in that chair of his and think about it . . . work it over in his mind. It's all psycho-fuckin-logical, you see. Why, if it'd been *you* that'd come out of the bushes by the light of the moon, he would have thought *you* was a wolf, Kenny."

Kenny laughs a little uneasily.

"Nope," Neary says gloomily. "Kid's testimony is just no damn good 'tall."

In his disgust and disappointment over the deposition taken from Marty Coslaw at the home of Marty's aunt and uncle in Stowe, Constable Neary has also overlooked this line: "Four of

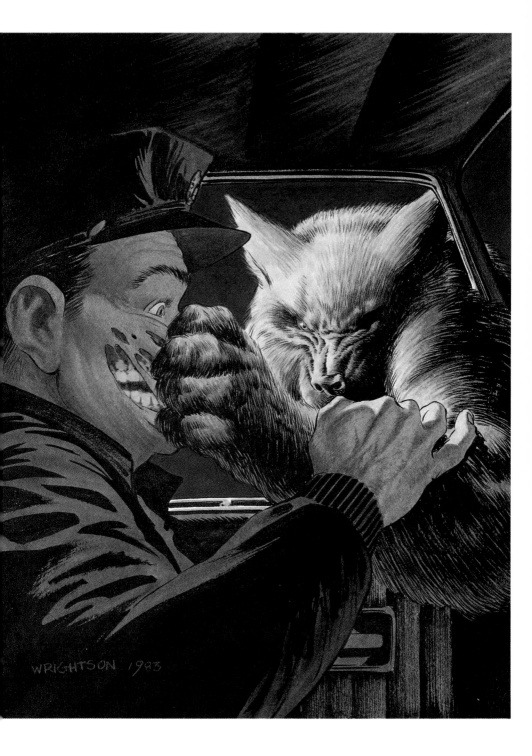

them went off at the side of his face—I guess you'd call it a face—all at once, and I guess maybe it put his eye out. His left eye."

If Constable Neary had chewed this over in his mind—and he hadn't—he would have laughed even more contemptuously, because in that hot, still August of 1984, there was only one townsperson sporting an eyepatch, and it was simply impossible to think of *that* person, of all persons, being the killer. Neary would have believed his mother the killer before he would have believed *that*.

"There's only one thing that'll solve this case," Constable Neary says, jabbing his finger at the four or five men sitting against the wall and waiting for their Saturday morning haircuts, "and that's good police work. And I intend to be the guy who does it. Those state Smokies are going to be laughing on the other side of their faces when I bring the guy in." Neary's face turns dreamy. "Anyone," he says. "A bank teller...gas jockey...just some guy you drink with down there at the bar. But good police-work will solve it. You mark my words."

But Constable Lander Neary's good police work comes to an end that night when a hairy, moon-silvered arm reaches through the open window of his Dodge pickup as he sits parked at the crossing-point of two dirt roads out in West Tarker's Mills. There is a low, snorting grunt, and a wild, terrifying smell— like something you would smell in the lion-house of a zoo.

His head is snapped around and he stares into one green eye. He sees the fur, the black, damp-looking snout. And when the snout wrinkles back, he sees the teeth. The beast claws at him almost playfully, and one of his cheeks is ripped away in a flap, exposing his teeth on the right side. Blood spouts everywhere. He can feel it running down over the shoulder of his shirt, sinking in warmly. He screams; he screams out of his mouth and out of his cheek. Over the beast's working shoulders, he can see the moon, flooding down white light.

He forgets all about his .30-.30 and the .45 strapped on

his belt. He forgets all about how this thing is psycho-fuckin-logical. He forgets all about good police work. Instead his mind fixes on something Kenny Franklin said in the barber-shop that morning. *Maybe it's some kind of disguise this fella puts on. Like a mask and all, you know.*

And so, as the werewolf reaches for Neary's throat, Neary reaches for its face, grabs double-handfuls of coarse, wiry fur and pulls, hoping madly that the mask will shift and then pull off—there will be the snap of an elastic, the liquid ripping sound of latex, and he will see the killer.

But nothing happens—nothing except a roar of pain and rage from the beast. It swipes at him with one clawed hand—yes, he can see it is a hand, however hideously misshapen, a *hand,* the boy was right—and lays his throat wide open. Blood jets over the truck's windshield and dashboard; it drips into the bottle of Busch that has been sitting tilted against Constable Neary's crotch.

The werewolf's other hand snags in Neary's freshly cut hair and yanks him half out of the Ford pick-up's cab. It howls once, in triumph, and then it buries its face and snout in Neary's neck. It feeds while the beer gurgles out of the spilled bottle and foams on the floor by the truck's brake and clutch pedals.

So much for psychology.

So much for good police work.

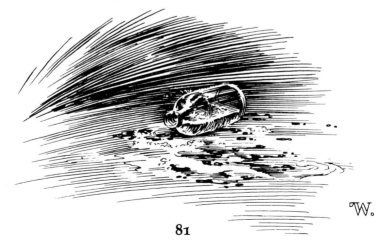

JANUARY
FEBRUARY
MARCH
APRIL
MAY
JUNE
JULY
AUGUST
SEPTEMBER
OCTOBER
NOVEMBER
DECEMBER

WRIGHTSON 1983

As the month wears on and the night of the full moon approaches again, the frightened people of Tarker's Mills wait for a break in the heat, but no such break comes. Elsewhere, in the wider world, the baseball divisional races are decided one by one and the football exhibition season has begun; in the Canadian Rockies, jolly old Willard Scott informs the people of Tarker's Mills, a foot of snow falls on the twenty-first of September. But in this corner of the world summer hangs right in there. Temperatures linger in the eighties during the days; kids, three weeks back in school and not happy to be there sit and swelter in droning classrooms where the clocks seem to have been set to click only one minute forward for each hour which passes in real time. Husbands and wives argue viciously for no reason, and at O'Neil's Gulf Station out on Town Road by the entrance to the turnpike, a tourist starts giving Pucky O'Neil some lip about the price of gas and Pucky brains the fellow with the gas-pump nozzle. The fellow, who is from New Jersey, needs four stitches in his upper lip and goes away muttering balefully under his breath about lawsuits and subpeonas.

"I don't know what he's bitching about," Pucky says sullenly that night in the Pub. "I only hit him with half of my force, you know? If I'd'a hit him with *all* my force, I woulda knocked his frockin smart mouth right the frock off. You know?"

"Sure," Billy Robertson says, because Pucky looks like he may hit *him* with all his force if he disagrees. "How about another beer, Puck?"

"Your frockin-A," Pucky says.

Milt Sturmfuller puts his wife in the hospital over a bit of egg that the dishwasher didn't take off one of the plates. He takes one look at that dried yellow smear on the plate she tried to give him for his lunch, and pounds her a good one. As Pucky O'Neil would have said, Milt hits her with all his force. "Damn slutty bitch," he says, standing over Donna Lee, who is sprawled out on the kitchen floor, her nose broken and bleeding, the back of her head also bleeding. "My mother used to get the dishes clean, and she didn't have no dishwasher, either. What's the matter with *you?"* Later, Milt will tell the doctor at the Portland General Hospital emergency room that Donna Lee fell down the back stairs. Donna Lee, terrorized and cowed after nine years in a marital war-zone, will back this up.

Around seven o'clock on the night of the full moon, a wind springs up—the first chill wind of that long summer season. It brings a rack of clouds from the north and for awhile the moon plays tag with these clouds, ducking in and out of them, turning their edges to beaten silver. Then the clouds grow thicker, and the moon disappears...yet it is there; the tides twenty miles out of Tarker's Mills feel its pull and so, closer to home, does the Beast.

Around two in the morning, a dreadful squealing arises from the pigpen of Elmer Zinneman on the West Stage Road, about twelve miles out of town. Elmer goes for his rifle, wearing only his pajama pants and his slippers. His wife, who was almost pretty when Elmer married her at sixteen in 1947, pleads and begs and cries, wanting him to stay with her, wanting him not to go out. Elmer shakes her off and grabs his gun from the entryway. His pigs are not just squealing; they are *screaming.* They sound like a bunch of very young girls surprised by a maniac at a slumber party. He is going, nothing can make him not go, he tells her...and then freezes with one work-callused hand on the latch of the back door as a screaming howl of triumph rises in the night. It is a wolf-cry, but there is something so human in the howl that it makes his hand drop from the latch and he allows Alice Zinneman to pull him back into the living room. He puts his arms around her and draws her down onto the sofa, and there they sit like two frightened children.

Now the crying of the pigs begins to falter and stop. Yes, they stop. One by one, they stop. Their squeals die in hoarse, bloody gargling sounds. The Beast howls again, its cry as silver as the moon. Elmer goes to the window and sees something—he cannot tell what—go bounding off into the deeper darkness.

The rain comes later, pelting against the windows as Elmer

and Alice sit up in bed together, all the lights in the bedroom on. It is a cold rain, the first real rain of the autumn, and tomorrow the first tinge of color will have come into the leaves.

Elmer finds what he expects in his pig-pen; carnage. All nine of his sows and both of his boars are dead—disembowelled and partly eaten. They lie in the mud, the cold rain pelting down on their carcasses, their bulging eyes staring up at the cold autumn sky.

Elmer's brother Pete, called over from Minot, stands beside Elmer. They don't speak for a long time, and then Elmer says what has been in Pete's mind as well. "Insurance will cover some of it. Not all, but some. I guess I can foot the rest. Better my pigs than another person."

Pete nods. "There's been enough," he says, his voice a murmur that can barely be heard over the rain.

"What do you mean?"

"You know what I mean. Next full moon there's got to be forty men out . . . or sixty . . . or a hundred and sixty. Time folks stopped dicking around and pretending it ain't happening, when any fool can see it is. Look here, for Christ's sweet sake!"

Pete points down. Around the slaughtered pigs, the soft earth of the pen is full of very large tracks. They look like the tracks of a wolf . . . but they also look weirdly human.

"You see those fucking tracks?"

"I see them," Elmer allows.

"You think Sweet Betsy from Pike made those tracks?"

"No. I guess not."

"Werewolf made those tracks," Pete says, "You know it, Alice knows it, most of the people in this town know it. Hell, even *I* know it, and I come from the next county over." He looks at his brother, his face dour and stern, the face of a New

England Puritan from 1650. And he repeats: "There's been enough. Time this thing was ended."

Elmer considers this long as the rain continues to tap on the two men's slickers, and then he nods. "I guess. But not next full moon."

"You want to wait until November?"

Elmer nods. "Bare woods. Better tracking, if we get a little snow."

"What about next month?"

Elmer Zinneman looks at his slaughtered pigs in the pen beside his barn. Then he looks at his brother Pete.

"People better look out," he says.

JANUARY
FEBRUARY
MARCH
APRIL
MAY
JUNE
JULY
AUGUST
SEPTEMBER
OCTOBER
NOVEMBER
DECEMBER

OCTOBER

WRIGHTSON /983

When Marty Coslaw comes home from trick or treating on Halloween Night with the batteries in his wheelchair all but dead flat, he goes directly to bed, where he lies awake until the half-moon rises in a cold sky strewn with stars like diamond chips. Outside, on the verandah where his life was saved by a string of Fourth of July firecrackers, a chill wind blows brown leaves in swirling, aimless corkscrews on the flagstones. They rattle like old bones. The October full moon has come and gone in Tarker's Mills with no new murder, the second month in a row this has happened. Some of the townspeople—Stan Pelky, the barber, is one, and Cal Blodwin, who owns Blodwin Chevrolet, the town's only car dealership, is another—believe that the terror is over; the killer was a drifter, or a tramp living out in the woods, and now he has moved on, just as they said he would. Others, however, are not so sure. These are the ones who do long reckoning on the four deer found slaughtered out by the turnpike the day after the October full moon, and upon Elmer Zinneman's eleven pigs, killed at full moon time in September. The argument rages at The Pub over beers during the long autumn nights.

But Marty Coslaw knows.

This night he has gone out trick or treating with his father (his father likes Halloween, likes the brisk cold, likes to laugh his hearty Big Pal laugh and bellow such idiotic things as "Hey, hey!" and "Ring-dang-doo!" when the doors open and familiar Tarker's Mills faces look out). Marty went as Yoda, a big rubber Don Post mask pulled down over his head and a voluminous robe on which covered his wasted legs. "You *always* get everything you want," Katie says with a toss of her head when she sees the mask . . . but he knows she isn't really mad at him (and as if to prove it, she makes him an artfully crooked Yoda staff to complete his getup), but perhaps sad because she is now considered too old to go out trick or treating. Instead she will go to a party with her junior high school friends. She will dance to Donna Summer records, and bob for apples, and later on the lights will be turned down for a game of spin-the-bottle and she will perhaps kiss some boy, not because she wants to but because it will be fun to giggle about it with her girlfriends in study hall the next day.

Marty's dad takes Marty in the van because the van has a built-in ramp he can use to get Marty in and out. Marty rolls down the ramp and then buzzes up and down the streets themselves in his chair. He carries his bag on his lap and they go to all the houses on their road and then to a few houses downtown: the Collinses, the MacInnes', the Manchesters', the Millikens', the Eastons'. There is a fishbowl full of candy corn inside The Pub. Snickers Bars at the Congregational Church parsonage and Chunky bars at the Baptist Parsonage. Then on to the Randolphs, the Quinns', the Dixons', and a dozen, two dozen more. Marty comes home with his bag of candy bulging . . . and a piece of scary, almost unbelievable knowledge.

He knows.

He knows who the werewolf is.

At one point on Marty's tour, the Beast himself, now safely between its moons of insanity, has dropped candy into his bag, unaware that Marty's face has gone deadly pale under his Don Post Yoda mask, or that, beneath his gloves, his fingers are clutching his Yoda staff so tightly that the fingernails are white. The werewolf smiles at Marty, and pats his rubber head.

But it is the werewolf. Marty knows, and not just because the man is wearing an eyepatch. There is something else— some vital similarity in this man's human face to the snarling face of the animal he saw on that silvery summer night almost four months ago now.

Since returning to Tarker's Mills from Vermont the day after Labor Day, Marty has kept a watch, sure that he will see the werewolf sooner or later, and sure that he will know him when he does because the werewolf will be a one-eyed man. Although the police nodded and said they would check it out when he told them he was pretty sure he had put out one of the were-

wolf's eyes, Marty could tell they didn't really believe him. Maybe that's because he is just a kid, or maybe it's because they weren't there on that July night when the confrontation took place. Either way, it doesn't matter. *He* knew it was so.

Tarker's Mills is a small town, but it is spread out, and until tonight Marty has not seen a one-eyed man, and he has not dared to ask questions; his mother is already afraid that the July episode may have permanently marked him. He is afraid that if he tries any out-and-out sleuthing it will eventually get back to her. Besides—Tarker's Mills is a small town. Sooner or later he will see the Beast with his human face on.

Going home, Mr. Coslaw (*Coach* Coslaw to his thousands of students, past and present) thinks Marty is so quiet because the evening and the excitement of the evening has tired him out. In truth, this is not so. Marty has never—except on the night of the wonderful bag of fireworks—felt so awake and alive. And his principal thought is this: it had taken him almost sixty days after returning home to discover the werewolf's identity because he, Marty, is a Catholic, and attends St. Mary's on the outskirts of town.

The man with the eyepatch, the man who dropped a Chunky bar into his bag and then smiled and patted him on top of his rubber head, is not a Catholic. Far from it. The Beast is the Reverend Lester Lowe, of the Grace Baptist Church.

Leaning out the door, smiling, Marty sees the eyepatch clearly in the yellow lamplight falling through the door; it gives the mousy little Reverend an almost piratical look.

"Sorry about your eye, Reverend Lowe," Mr. Coslaw said in his booming Big Pal voice. "Hope it's nothing serious?"

The Rev. Lowe's smile grew longsuffering. Actually, he said, he had lost the eye. A benign tumor; it had been necessary to remove the eye to get at the tumor. But it was the Lord's will, and he was adjusting well. He had patted the top of Marty's whole-head mask again and said that some he knew had heavier crosses to bear.

So now Marty lies in his bed, listening to the October wind sing outside, rattling the season's last leaves, hooting dimly through the eyeholes of the carven pumpkins which flank the Coslaw driveway, watching the half-moon ride the star-studded sky. The question is this: *What is he to do now?*

He doesn't know, but he feels sure that in time the answer will come.

He sleeps the deep, dreamless sleep of the very young, while outside the river of wind blows over Tarker's Mills, washing out October and bringing in cold, star-shot November, autumn's iron month.

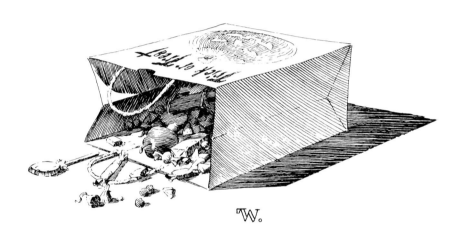

JANUARY
FEBRUARY
MARCH
APRIL
MAY
JUNE
JULY
AUGUST
SEPTEMBER
OCTOBER
NOVEMBER
DECEMBER

NOVEMBER

WRIGHTSON

The smoking butt end of the year, November's dark iron, has come to Tarker's Mills. A strange exodus seems to be taking place on Main Street. The Rev. Lester Lowe watches it from the door of the Baptist Parsonage; he has just come out to get his mail and he holds six circulars and one single letter in his hand, watching the conga-line of dusty pick-up trucks—Fords and Chevys and International Harvesters—snake its way out of town.

Snow is coming, the weatherman says, but these are no riders before the storm, bound for warmer climes; you don't head out for Florida or California's golden shore with your hunting jacket on and your gun behind you in the cab rack and your dogs in the flatbed. This is the fourth day that the men, led by Elmer Zinneman and his brother Pete, have headed out with dogs and guns and a great many six-packs of beer. It is a fad that has caught on as the full moon approaches. Bird season's over, deer season, too. But it's still open season on werewolves, and most of these men, behind the mask of their grim get-the-wagons-in-a-circle faces, are having a great time. As Coach Coslaw might has said, Doodly-damn right!

Some of the men, Rev. Lowe knows, are doing no more than skylarking; here is a chance to get out in the woods, pull beers, piss in ravines, tell jokes about polacks and frogs and niggers, shoot at squirrels and crows. *They're the real animals*, Lowe thinks, his hand unconsciously going to the eyepatch he has worn since July. *Somebody will shoot somebody, most likely. They're lucky it hasn't happened already.*

The last of the trucks drives out of sight over Tarker's Hill, horn honking, dogs yarking and barking in the back. Yes, some of the men are just skylarking, but some—Elmer and Pete Zinneman, for example—are dead serious.

If that creature, man or beast or whatever it is, goes hunting this month, the dogs will pick up its scent, the Rev. Lowe has heard Elmer say in the barber shop not two weeks ago. *And if it—or he—don't go out, then maybe we'll have saved a life. Someone's livestock at the very least.*

Yes, there are some of them—maybe a dozen, maybe two dozen—who mean business. But it is not them that has brought this strange new feeling into the back of Lowe's brain—that sense of being brought to bay.

It's the notes that have done that. The notes, the longest of them only two sentences long, written in a childish, laborious hand, sometimes misspelled. He looks down at the letter that has come in today's mail, addressed in that same childish script, addressed as the others have been addressed: *The Reverend Lowe, Baptist Parsonage, Tarker's Mills, Maine 04491.*

Now, this strange, trapped feeling . . . the way he imagines a fox must feel when it realizes that the dogs have somehow chased it into a cul-de-sac. That panicked moment that the fox turns, its teeth bared, to do battle with the dogs that will surely pull it to pieces.

He closes the door firmly, goes inside to the parlor where the grandfather clock ticks solemn ticks and tocks solemn tocks; he sits down, puts the religious circulars carefully aside on the table Mrs. Miller polishes twice a week, and opens his new letter. Like the others, there is no salutation. Like the others, it is unsigned. Written in the center of a sheet torn from a grade-schooler's lined notepad, is this sentence:

Why don't you kill yourself?

The Rev. Lowe puts a hand to his forehead—it trembles slightly. With the other hand he crumples the sheet of paper up and puts it in the large glass ashtray in the center of the table (Rev. Lowe does all of his counselling in the parlor, and some of his troubled parishoners smoke). He takes a book of matches from his Saturday afternoon "at home" sweater and lights the note, as he has lit the others. He watches it burn.

Lowe's knowledge of what he is has come in two distinct stages: Following his nightmare in May, the dream in which everyone in the Old Home Sunday congregation turned into a werewolf, and following his terrible discovery of Clyde Corliss's

gutted body, he has begun to realize that something is ... well, wrong with him. He knows no other way to put it. Something *wrong*. But he also knows that on some mornings, usually during the period when the moon is full, he awakes feeling amazingly *good*, amazingly *well*, amazingly *strong*. This feeling ebbs with the moon, and then grows again with the next moon.

Following the dream and Corliss's death, he has been forced to acknowledge other things, which he had, up until then, been able to ignore. Clothes that are muddy and torn. Scratches and bruises he cannot account for (but since they never hurt or ache, as ordinary scratches and bruises do, they have been easy to dismiss, to simply ... not think about). He has even been able to ignore the traces of blood he has sometimes found on his hands ... and lips.

Then, on July 5th, the second stage. Simply described: he had awakened blind in one eye. As with the cuts and scratches, there had been no pain; simply a gored, blasted socket where his left eye had been. At that point the knowledge had become too great for denial: *he* is the werewolf; *he* is the Beast.

For the last three days he has felt familiar sensations: a great restlessness, an impatience that is almost joyful, a sense of tension in his body. It is coming again—the change is almost here again. Tonight the moon will rise full, and the hunters will be out with their dogs. Well, no matter. He is smarter than they give him credit for. They speak of a man-wolf, but think only in terms of the wolf, not the man. They can drive in their pickups, and he can drive in his small Volare sedan. And this afternoon he will drive down Portland way, he thinks, and stay at some motel on the outskirts of town. And if the change comes, there will be no hunters, no dogs. *They* are not the ones who frighten him.

Why don't you kill yourself?

The first note came early this month. It said simply:

I know who you are.

The second said:

110

If you are a man of God, get out of town. Go someplace where there are animals for you to kill but no people.

The third said:

End it.

That was all; just *End it.* And now

Why don't you kill yourself?

Because I don't want to, the Rev. Lowe thinks petulantly. *This—whatever it is—is nothing I asked for. I wasn't bitten by a wolf or cursed by a gypsy. It just . . . happened. I picked some flowers for the vases in the church vestry one day last November. Up by that pretty little cemetery on Sunshine Hill. I never saw such flowers before . . . and they were dead before I could get back to town. They turned black, every one. Perhaps that was when it started to happen. No reason to think so, exactly . . . but I do. And I won't kill myself. They are the animals, not me.*

Who is writing the notes?

He doesn't know. The attack on Marty Coslaw has not been reported in the weekly Tarker's Mills newspapers, and he prides himself on not listening to gossip. Also, as Marty did not know about Lowe until Halloween because their religious circles do not touch, the Rev. Lowe does not know about Marty. And he has no memory of what he does in his beast-state; only that alcoholic sense of well-being when the cycle has finished for another month, and the restlessness before.

I am a man of God, he thinks, getting up and beginning to pace, walking faster and faster in the quiet parlor where the grandfather clock ticks solemn ticks and tocks solemn tocks. *I am a man of God and I will not kill myself. I do good here, and if I sometimes do evil, why, men have done evil before me; evil also serves the will of God, or so the Book of Job teaches us; if I have been cursed from Outside, then God will bring me down in His time. All things serve the will of God . . . and who is he? Shall I make inquiries? Who was attacked on July 4th? How did I (it) lose his (its) eye? Perhaps he should be silenced . . . but not this month. Let them put their dogs back in their kennels first. Yes . . .*

111

He begins to walk faster and faster, bent low, unaware that his beard, usually scant (he can get away with only shaving once every three days . . . at the right time of the month, that is), has now sprung out thick and scruffy and wiry, and that his one brown eye has gone a hazel shade that is deepening moment by moment toward the emerald green it will become later this night. He is hunching forward as he walks, and he has begun to talk to himself . . . but the words are growing lower and lower, more and more like growls.

At last, as the gray November afternoon tightens down toward an early anvil-colored dusk, he bounds into the kitchen, snatches the Volare's keys from the peg by the door, and almost runs toward the car. He drives toward Portland fast, smiling, and he does not slow when the season's first snow starts to skirl into the beams of his headlights, dancers from the iron sky. He senses the moon somewhere above the clouds; he senses its power; his chest expands, straining the seams of his white shirt.

He tunes the radio to a rock and roll station, and he feels *just . . . great!*

And what happens later that night might be a judgment from God, or a jest of those older gods that men worshipped from the safety of stone circles on moonlit nights—oh, it's funny, all right, pretty funny, because Lowe has gone all the way to Portland to become the Beast, and the man he ends up ripping open on that snowy November night is Milt Sturmfuller, a lifelong resident of Tarker's Mills . . . and perhaps God is just after all, because if there is a first-class grade-A shit in Tarker's Mills, it is Milt Sturmfuller. He has come in this night as he has on other nights, telling his battered wife Donna Lee that he is on business, but his business is a B-girl named Rita Tennison who has given him a lively case of herpes which Milt has already passed on to Donna Lee, who has never so much as looked at another man in all the years they have been married.

The Rev. Lowe has checked into a motel called The Driftwood near the Portland-Westbrook line, and this is the same motel that Milt Sturmfuller and Rita Tennison have chosen on this November night to do their business.

Milt steps out at quarter past ten to retrieve a bottle of bourbon he's left in the car, and he is in fact congratulating himself on being far from Tarker's Mills on the night of the full moon when the one-eyed Beast leaps on him from the roof of a snow-shrouded Peterbilt ten-wheeler and takes his head off with one gigantic swipe. The last sound Milt Sturmfuller hears in his life is the werewolf's rising snarl of triumph; his head rolls under the Peterbilt, the eyes wide, the neck spraying blood, and the bottle of bourbon drops from his jittering hand as the Beast buries its snout in his neck and begins to feed.

And the next day, back in the Baptist parsonage in Tarker's Mills and feeling *just . . . great,* the Rev. Lowe will read the account of the murder in the newspaper and think piously: *He was not a good man. All things serve the Lord.*

And following this, he will think: *Who is the kid sending the notes? Who was it in July? It's time to find out. It's time to listen to some gossip.*

The Rev. Lester Lowe readjusts his eyepatch, shakes out a new section of the newspaper and thinks: *All things serve the Lord, if it's the Lord's will, I'll find him. And silence him. Forever.*

JANUARY
FEBRUARY
MARCH
APRIL
MAY
JUNE
JULY
AUGUST
SEPTEMBER
OCTOBER
NOVEMBER
DECEMBER

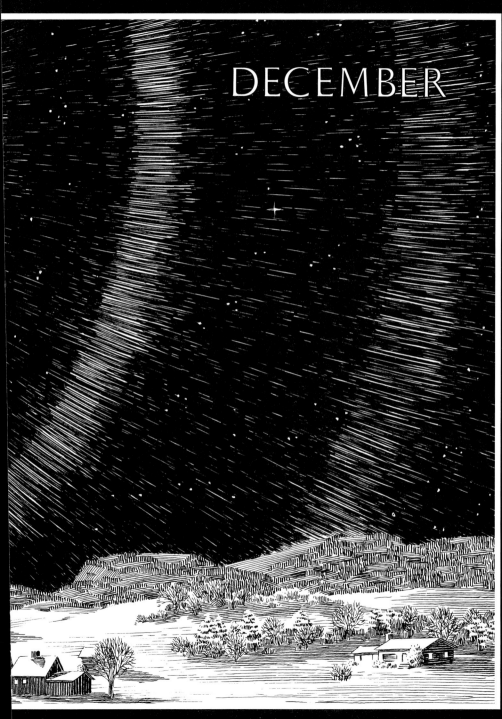

It is fifteen minutes of midnight on New Year's Eve. In Tarker's Mills, as in the rest of the world, the year is drawing to its close, and in Tarker's Mills as in the rest of the world, the year has brought changes.

Milt Sturmfuller is dead and his wife Donna Lee, at last free of her bondage, has moved out of town. Gone to Boston, some say; gone to Los Angeles, other say. Another woman has tried to make a go of the Corner Bookshop and failed, but the barber shop, The Market Basket, and The Pub are doing business at the same old places, thank you very much. Clyde Corliss is dead, but his two goodfornothing brothers, Alden and Errol, are still alive and well and cashing in their foodstamps at the A&P two towns over—they don't quite have the nerve to do it right here in the Mills. Gramma Hague, who used to make the best pies in Tarker's Mills, has died of a heart attack, Willie Harrington, who is ninety-two, slipped on the ice in front of his little house on Ball Street late in November and broke his hip, but the library has received a nice bequest in the will of a wealthy summer resident, and next year construction will begin on the children's wing that has been talked about in town meeting since time out of mind. Ollie Parker, the school principal, had a nosebleed that just wouldn't quit in October and is diagnosed as an acute hypertensive. *Lucky you didn't blow your brains out*, the doctor grunted, unwrapping the blood-pressure cuff, and told Ollie to lose forty pounds. For a wonder, Ollie loses twenty of those pounds by Christmas. He looks and feels like a new man. "*Acts* like a new man, too," his wife tells her close friend Delia Burney, with a lecherous little grin. Brady Kincaid, killed by the Beast in kite-flying season, is still dead. And Marty Coslaw, who used to sit right behind Brady in school, is still a cripple.

Things change, things don't change, and, in Tarker's Mills, the year is ending as the year came in—a howling blizzard is roaring outside, and the Beast is around. Somewhere.

Sitting in the living room of the Coslaw home and watching Dick Clark's Rockin New Year's Eve are Marty Coslaw and his

119

Uncle Al. Uncle Al is on the couch. Marty is sitting in his wheelchair in front of the TV. There is a gun in Marty's lap, a .38 Colt Woodsman. Two bullets are chambered in the gun, and both of them are pure silver. Uncle Al has gotten a friend of his from Hampden, Mac McCutcheon, to make them in a bullet-loader. This Mac McCutcheon, after some protests, has melted Marty's silver confirmation spoon down with a propane torch, and calibrated the weight of powder needed to propel the bullets without sending them into a wild spin. "I don't guarantee they'll work," this Mac McCutcheon has told Uncle Al, "but they probably will. What you gonna kill, Al? A were-wolf or a vampire?"

"One of each," Uncle Al says, giving him his grin right back. "That's why I got you to make two. There was a banshee hanging around as well, but his father died in North Dakota and he had to catch a plane to Fargo." They have a laugh over that, and then Al says: "They're for a nephew of mine. He's crazy over movie monsters, and I thought they'd make an interesting Christmas present for him."

"Well, if he fires one into a batten, bring it back to the shop," Mac tells him. "I'd like to see what happens."

In truth, Uncle Al doesn't know what to think. He hadn't seen Marty or been to Tarker's Mills since July 3rd; as he could have predicted, his sister, Marty's mother, is furious with him about the fireworks. *He could have been killed, you stupid asshole! What in the name of God did you think you were doing?* she shouts down the telephone wire at him.

Sounds like it was the fireworks that saved his—Al begins, but there is the sharp click of a broken connection in his ear. His sister is stubborn; when she doesn't want to hear something, she won't.

Then, early this month, a call came from Marty. "I have to see you, Uncle Al," Marty said. "You're the only one I can talk to."

"I'm in the doghouse with our mom, kid," Al answered.

"It's important," Marty said. "Please. *Please."*

So he came, and he braved his sister's icy, disapproving silence, and on a cold, clear early December day, Al took Marty for a ride in his sports car, loading him carefully into the passenger bucket. Only this day there was no speeding and no wild laughter; only Uncle Al listening as Marty talked. Uncle Al listened with growing disquiet as the tale is told.

Marty began by telling Al again about the night of the wonderful bag of fireworks, and how he had blown out the creature's left eye with the Black Cat firecrackers. Then he told him about Halloween, and the Rev. Lowe. Then he told Uncle Al that he had begun sending the Rev. Lowe anonymous notes ... anonymous, that is, until the last two, following the murder of Milt Sturmfuller in Portland. Those he signed just as he had been taught in English class: *Yours truly, Martin Coslaw.*

"You shouldn't have sent the man notes, anonymous or otherwise!" Uncle Al said sharply. "Christ, Marty! Did it ever occur to you that you could be *wrong?"*

"Sure it did," Marty said. "That's why I signed my name to the last two. Aren't you going to ask me what happened? Aren't you going to ask me if he called up my father and told him I'd sent him a note saying why don't you kill yourself and another one saying we're closing in on you?"

"He didn't do that, did he?" Al asked, knowing the answer already.

"No," Marty said quietly. "He hasn't talked to my dad, and he hasn't talked to my mom, and he hasn't talked to me."

"Marty, there could be a hundred reasons for th—"

"No. There's only *one.* He's the werewolf, he's the Beast, it's *him,* and he's waiting for the full moon. As the Reverend Lowe, he can't do anything. But as the werewolf, he can do plenty. He can shut me up."

And Marty spoke with such chilling simplicity that Al was almost convinced. "So what do you want from me?" Al asked.

Marty told him. He wanted two silver bullets, and a gun to shoot them with, and he wanted Uncle Al to come over on New Year's Eve, the night of the full moon.

"I'll do no such thing," Uncle Al said. "Marty, you're a good kid, but you're going loopy. I think you've come down with a good case of Wheelchair Fever. If you think it over, you'll know it."

"Maybe," Marty said. "But think how you'll feel if you get a call on New Year's Day saying I'm dead in my bed, chewed to pieces? Do you want that on your conscience, Uncle Al?"

Al started to speak, then closed his mouth with a snap. He turned into a driveway, hearing the Mercedes' front wheels crunch in the new snow. He reversed and started back. He fought in Viet Nam and won a couple of medals there; he had successfully avoided lengthy entanglements with several lusty young ladies; and now he felt caught and trapped by his ten-year-old nephew. His *crippled* ten-year-old nephew. Of course he didn't want such a thing on his conscience—not even the *possibility* of such a thing. And Marty knew it. As Marty knew that if Uncle Al thought there was even one chance in a thousand that he might be right—

Four days later, on December 10th, Uncle Al called. "Great news!" Marty announced to his family, wheeling his chair back into the family room. "Uncle Al's coming over for New Year's Eve!"

"He certainly is *not*," his mother says in her coldest, brusquest tone.

Marty was not daunted. "Gee, sorry—I already invited him," he said. "He said he'd bring party-powder for the fireplace."

His mother had spent the rest of the day glaring at Marty every time she looked in his direction or he in hers...but she didn't call her brother back and tell him to stay away, and that was the most important thing.

At supper that night Katie whispered hissingly in his ear: "You *always* get what you want! Just because you're a cripple!"

Grinning, Marty whispered back: "I love you too, sis."

"You little *booger!*"

She flounced away.

And here it is, New Year's Eve. Marty's mother was sure Al wouldn't show up as the storm intensified, the wind howling and moaning and driving snow before it. Truth to tell, Marty has had a few bad moments himself...but Uncle Al arrived up around eight, driving not his Mercedes sports car but a borrowed four-wheel drive.

By eleven-thirty, everyone in the family has gone to bed except for the two of them, which is pretty much as Marty had foreseen things. And although Uncle Al is still pooh-poohing the whole thing, he has brought not one but two handguns concealed under his heavy CPO coat. The one with the two silver bullets he hands wordlessly to Marty after the family has gone to bed (as if to complete making the point, Marty's mother slammed the door of the bedroom she shares with Marty's dad when she went to bed—slammed it hard). The other is filled with more conventional lead-loads...but Al reckons that if a crazyman is going to break in here tonight (and as time passes and nothing happens, he comes to doubt that more and more), the .45 Magnum will stop him.

Now, on the TV, they are switching the cameras more and more often to the big lighted ball on top of the Allied Chemical Building in Times Square. The last few minutes of the year are running out. The crowd cheers. In the corner opposite the TV, the Coslaw Christmas tree still stands, drying out now, getting a little brown, looking sadly denuded of its presents.

"Marty, nothing—" Uncle Al begins, and then the big picture window in the family room blows inward in a twinkle of glass,

124

letting in the howling black wind from outside, twisting skirls of white snow ... and the Beast.

Al is frozen for a moment, utterly frozen with horror and disbelief. It is huge, this Beast, perhaps seven feet tall, although it is hunched over so that its front hand-paws almost drag on the rug. Its one green eye *(just like Marty said,* he thinks numbly, *all of it, just like Marty said)* glares around with a terrible, rolling sentience ... and fixes upon Marty, sitting in his wheelchair. It leaps at the boy, a rolling howl of triumph exploding out of its chest and past its huge yellow-white teeth.

Calmly, his face hardly changing, Marty raises the .38 pistol. He looks very small in his wheelchair, his legs like sticks inside his soft and faded jeans, his fur-lined slippers on feet that have been numb and senseless all of his life. And, incredibly, over the werewolf's mad howling, over the wind's screaming, over the clap and clash of his own tottering thoughts about how this can possibly be in a world of real people and real things, over all of this Al hears his nephew say: "Poor old Reverend Lowe. I'm gonna try to set you free."

And as the werewolf leaps, its shadow a blob on the carpet, its claw-tipped hands outstretched, Marty fires. Because of the lower powder-load, the gun makes an almost absurdly insignificant pop. It sounds like a Daisy air-rifle.

But the werewolf's roar of rage spirals up into an even higher register, a lunatic screech of pain now. It crashes into the wall and its shoulder punches a hole right through to the other side. A Currier and Ives painting falls onto its head, skates down the thick pelt of its back and shatters as the werewolf turns. Blood is pouring down the savage, hairy mask of its face, and its green eye seems rolling and confused. It staggers toward Marty, growling, its claw-hands opening and closing, its snapping jaws cutting off wads of blood-streaked foam. Marty holds the gun in both hands, as a small child holds his drinking cup.

He waits, waits . . . and as the werewolf lunges again, he fires. Magically, the beast's other eye blows out like a candle in a stormwind! It screams again and staggers, now blind, toward the window. The blizzard riffles the curtains and twists them around its head—Al can see flowers of blood begin to bloom on the white cloth—as, on the TV, the big lighted ball begins to descend its pole.

The werewolf collapses to its knees as Marty's dad, wild-eyed and dressed in bright yellow pajamas, dashes into the room. The .45 Magnum is still in Al's lap. He has never so much as raised it.

Now the beast collapses . . . shudders once . . . and dies.

Mr. Coslaw stares at it, open-mouthed.

Marty turnes to Uncle Al, the smoking gun in his hands. His face looks tired . . . but at peace.

"Happy New Year, Uncle Al," he says, "it's dead. The Beast is dead." And then he begins to weep.

On the floor, under the mesh of Mrs. Coslaw's best white curtains, the werewolf has begun to change. The hair which has shagged its face and body seems to be *pulling in* somehow. The lips, drawn back in a snarl of pain and fury, relax and cover the shrinking teeth. The claws melt magically away to finger-nails . . . fingernails that have been almost pathetically gnawed and bitten.

The Reverend Lester Lowe lies there, wrapped in a bloody shroud of curtain, snow blowing around him in random patterns.

Uncle Al goes to Marty and comforts him as Marty's dad gawks down at the naked body on the floor and as Marty's mother, clutching the neck of her robe, creeps into the room. Al hugs Marty tight, tight, tight.

"You done good, kid," he whispers. "I love you."

Outside, the wind howls and screams against the snow-filled sky, and in Tarker's Mills, the first minute of the new year becomes history.

Afterword

Any dedicated moon-watcher will know that, regardless of the year, I have taken a good many liberties with the lunar cycle—usually to take advantage of days (Valentine's, July 4th, etc.) which "mark" certain months in our minds. To those readers who feel that I didn't know any better, I assert that I did . . . but the temptation was simply too great to resist.

Stephen King
August 4, 1983